PUFFIN BOOKS

Pink for
Polar Bear

Other titles in the First Young Puffin series

BEAR'S BAD MOOD John Prater
BELLA AT THE BALLET Brian Ball
BLESSU Dick King-Smith
BUBBLEGUM BOTHER Wendy Smith
THE DAY THE SMELLS WENT WRONG Catherine Sefton
THE DAY WE BRIGHTENED UP THE SCHOOL
Mick Gowar
DIZ AND THE BIG FAT BURGLAR
Margaret Stuart Barry
DUMPLING Dick King-Smith
ERIC'S ELEPHANT GOES CAMPING John Gatehouse
ERIC'S ELEPHANT ON HOLIDAY John Gatehouse
FETCH THE SLIPPER Sheila Lavelle
GERALDINE GETS LUCKY Robert Leeson
GOODNIGHT, MONSTER Carolyn Dinan
HAPPY CHRISTMAS, RITA! Hilda Offen
HARRY'S AUNT Sheila Lavelle
HOP IT, DUGGY DOG! Brian Ball
THE INCREDIBLE SHRINKING HIPPO Stephanie Baudet
THE JEALOUS GIANT Kaye Umansky
NINA THE GOBBLEDEGOAT Penny Ives
THE POCKET ELEPHANT Catherine Sefton
RAJ IN CHARGE Andrew and Diana Davies
RITA THE RESCUER Hilda Offen
THE ROMANTIC GIANT Kaye Umansky
SOS FOR RITA Hilda Offen
WHAT STELLA SAW Wendy Smith
WOOLLY JUMPERS Peta Blackwell

Pink for Polar Bear

Written and illustrated by

Valerie Solís

PUFFIN BOOKS

PUFFIN BOOKS

Published by the Penguin Group
Penguin Books Ltd, 27 Wrights Lane, London W8 5TZ, England
Penguin Putnam Inc., 375 Hudson Street, New York, New York 10014, USA
Penguin Books Australia Ltd, Ringwood, Victoria, Australia
Penguin Books Canada Ltd, 10 Alcorn Avenue, Toronto, Ontario, Canada M4V 3B2
Penguin Books (NZ) Ltd, 182–190 Wairau Road, Auckland 10, New Zealand

Penguin Books Ltd, Registered Offices: Harmondsworth, Middlesex, England

First published by Hamish Hamilton Ltd 1996
Published in Puffin Books 1998
1 3 5 7 9 10 8 6 4 2

Filmset in Plantin

Made and printed in Hong Kong by Imago Publishing Limited

British Library Cataloguing in Publication Data
A CIP catalogue record for this book is available from the British Library

ISBN 0–140–38837–0

Nanook the polar bear was not white like
her brother and sister. Her fur was pink.

Some of the big polar bears said that
Nanook was different because she had been
born at sunset. They thought the sun's pink
rays had coloured her fur. Her family
called her Nanook, the "daughter of the
setting sun".

"Who has ever heard of a pink polar bear?" said a very large and curious bear. The other bears laughed.

Nanook felt sad and lonely. She very much wanted to be a white polar bear like all the others.

"Maybe, I am not a real polar bear at all?" she thought sadly. "Polar bears love to chase seals, swim and catch fish. I don't like chasing the poor seals, and I'm not much good at swimming or catching fish."

One day a terrific snowstorm blew up as Nanook and her family were coming home after a day's fishing.

The wind howled and raged all over the North Pole. The snow fell so thickly that Nanook couldn't see a thing as she struggled to keep up with her family.

"I'm so tired. The wind is far too strong. Perhaps I should rest and catch up with the others later," she thought.

Nanook curled up in the snow and before long she fell into a deep sleep.

The next morning, Nanook awoke to find herself covered with snow.

"Oh dear! I must have slept for hours!" she thought.

Then she realized that she was all alone on an iceberg floating out to sea.

"Oh no! My family will never find me now!" she exclaimed.

Nanook floated further and further out to sea. Soon she began to feel very hungry.

She thought for hours about jumping into the sea to catch a fish, but the rough waves frightened her.

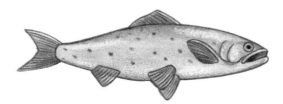

Suddenly, Nanook heard a cry above her.

A beautiful plump fish dropped out of the sky at her feet.

Nanook looked up and saw Gullak, the seagull.

"Oh, thank you a million times, Gullak, thank you!" shouted Nanook.

"You're welcome," replied Gullak.

Every day, Gullak caught the biggest
and best fish for Nanook.

Gullak was a great storyteller as well as a
great friend.

Nanook loved to listen to his tales about
mermaids, flying fish, singing humpback
whales, shipwrecks and many other
fantastic things he had seen in his lifetime.

Nanook missed Gullak a lot when he wasn't around. There was nothing much to do on an iceberg except count other icebergs. Sometimes, Nanook saw some seals or walruses but they were either sleeping or too far away to hear her.

One night, beautiful melodies echoed all over the North Pole, waking Nanook from her dreams.

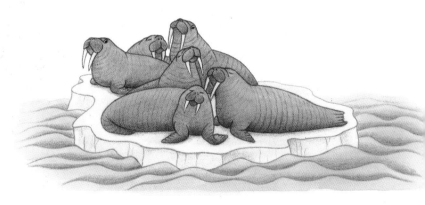

It was the singing humpback whales!

Suddenly, a great spray of water blew high into the air and a family of whales appeared near Nanook's iceberg.

"You must be the humpback whales that Gullak talks about!" cried Nanook. "Your songs are beautiful! I wish I could sing like you and be heard far away. Then I would never be lonely."

"And so you shall," replied the largest whale called Fluke. "We give you the 'gift of song'. From now on, you will be able to talk to us by singing, no matter how far away we are. You will never feel lonely again, Nanook, daughter of the setting sun."

Then music filled Nanook's heart and she burst into song. Her voice was as sweet as a nightingale.

The delighted whales blew great
fountains of water into the air to show their
pleasure, and set off on their long journey
to other seas.

From that moment Nanook never
stopped singing.

She sang to the humpback whales as they
travelled to distant seas. The starry skies
echoed with her sweet songs.

Nanook, the daughter of the setting sun, was talked about all over the North Pole and beyond.

Seals, seagulls and walruses travelled many miles just to hear her sing. Nanook was very happy.

One day Nanook had a great surprise.

A large iceberg was floating silently towards her.

"Ahoy, there!" a voice called out.

Nanook stopped singing.

"Hello!" she called back. But she could see nothing through the heavily falling snow.

"Ahoy, there!" the mysterious voice shouted again.

This time it came from right beside her.

"A blue polar bear!" exclaimed Nanook, peering through the snow.

"Hello, Nanook, daughter of the setting sun," said the bear.

"Hello, but how do you know my name?" she asked.

"Ah! Nanook, the Singing Bear is famous throughout the North Pole," answered the bear as he jumped onto Nanook's iceberg.

"Really?" And who are you?" asked Nanook.

"My name is Koonan, son of the midday sky. I have been travelling on this iceberg for a long time listening to your enchanting music. Your voice is so beautiful that I closed my eyes and made a wish. And now I am here," said Koonan.

"What was your wish?" asked Nanook.

"I wished with all my heart that you would sing especially for me," replied Koonan.

"Of course," she said, delighted. "I shall sing the sweetest song of all just for you, Koonan."

Koonan threw his arms into the air with joy and began to dance gracefully.

"Auuk, auuk!"

There was a cry above them.

Gullak dropped two plump fish to celebrate the beginning of a special friendship.

Nanook thought she was so lucky to have such marvellous friends.

Gullak had fed her and told her tales, and the whales had given her a wonderful gift of song. Now she had found Koonan, a very special bear friend.

"I'm glad I am me. I don't mind if I'm not a real polar bear after all," she said.

"What do you mean?" asked Koonan. "You look exactly like a polar bear to me. A very colourful polar bear."

Nanook thought for a few moments.
The setting sun's rays turned her fur
even pinker.

"Yes," she said. "And so are you!"

And together they laughed with
happiness.

Also available in First Young Puffin

ERIC'S ELEPHANT ON HOLIDAY
John Gatehouse

When Eric and his family go on holiday to the
seaside, Eric's elephant goes too. Everyone is
surprised – and rather cross – to find a big white
elephant on the beach. But the elephant soon
amazes them with her jumbo tricks and makes it a
very special holiday indeed!

THE JEALOUS GIANT
Kaye Umansky

Waldo the giant is jealous! Heavy Hetty has a
handsome new wrestling trainer and she doesn't
have time to cook Waldo delicious meals any more.
Waldo decides to impress Hetty with his own
cooking skills – but it's a lot harder than he thinks!

WHAT STELLA SAW
Wendy Smith

Stella's mum is a fortune-teller who always gets
things wrong. But when football-mad Stella starts
reading tea-leaves, she seems to be right every time!
Or is she . . .